The Christmas Sweater

For my grandfather, who taught me to see magic everywhere —*glenn*

For the Koontz family of Enumclaw —*brandon*

ALADDIN/Mercury Radio Arts, Inc.

An imprint of Simon & Schuster Children's Publishing Division

1230 Avenue of the Americas, New York, NY 10020

First Aladdin/Mercury Radio Arts hardcover edition October 2009

Text copyright © 2008, 2009 by Mercury Radio Arts, Inc.

Illustrations copyright © 2009 by Brandon Dorman

For information about special discounts for bulk purchases, please contact Simon & Schuster Special Sales

at 1-866-506-1949 or business@simonandschuster.com.

The Simon & Schuster Speakers Bureau can bring authors to your live event. For more information or

to book an event contact the Simon & Schuster Speakers Bureau at 1-866-248-3049 or visit our website at simonspeakers.com.

Designed by Karin Paprocki

The text of this book was set in Wade Sans Light Plain.

The illustrations for this book were rendered digitally.

Manufactured in the United States of America

2 4 6 8 10 9 7 5 3 1

Library of Congress Cataloging-in-Publication Data

Beck, Glenn.

The Christmas sweater : a picture book / by Glenn Beck ; illustrated by Brandon Dorman. — 1st Aladdin hardcover ed.   p. cm.

Picture book version of a novel of the same name first published in 2008.

Summary: More than anything, Eddie wants a bicycle for Christmas, but his grandfather shows him the magic there can be in a simple gift made with love.

ISBN 978-1-4169-9543-2 (hardcover)

[1. Gifts—Fiction. 2. Sweaters—Fiction. 3. Grandfathers—Fiction. 4. Christmas—Fiction.]   I. Dorman, Brandon, ill. II. Title.

PZ7.B3807678Chr 2010   [E]—dc22   2009015490

The Christmas Sweater

A PICTURE BOOK

Illustrated by
Brandon Dorman

Adapted by
Chris Schoebinger

Original story by

GLENN BECK with

KEVIN BALFE and JASON WRIGHT

ALADDIN/MERCURY RADIO ARTS, INC.
New York London Toronto Sydney

ON CHRISTMAS EVE, Eddie shook his snow globe one last time and placed it on the dresser beside his bed. He watched the snowstorm swirl and thought about the one gift he wanted most for Christmas—a new bicycle. As the final snowflakes drifted away, he heard a soft knock at his door.

Eddie turned and saw his
grandfather tiptoeing into the room. He was wearing
his favorite fluffy red hat——a hat that used to make Eddie think his
grandfather was Santa Claus himself.

"What did you find, Grandpa? Am I getting the bike I want?" he asked.

Grandpa looked around to make sure they were alone. Then he whispered, "Well, I snooped around the house and I have good news and bad news. What do you want first?"

"Hmm." Eddie frowned. "You'd better give me the bad news first."

Grandpa cleared his throat.

"The bad news is that I didn't find a bike."

Eddie's heart sank. He knew that children don't always get what they want for Christmas, but he'd tried to be extra good all year long. "Don't I deserve a bike?" he thought to himself. Eddie's head fell back onto his pillow. He looked up at the stars on his ceiling and mumbled, "So, what's the good news?"

"Ah, yes." Grandpa's eyes lit up. "The good news is that you're getting a Christmas sweater."

"Huh?" Eddie sat up in disbelief. "A Christmas sweater? That's the good news? A boring, useless, itchy sweater? I don't want ANY sweater, but especially not a Christmas sweater!"

"Shhhhhh!" Grandpa hushed him. "Eddie, sometimes a sweater isn't just a sweater. I still remember the year my mother knitted one for me. It brought me magic for years and years. Still does. See, when a gift is made by hand, all of that person's love is captured in it. Once they give it to you, that love turns into Christmas magic. . . ."

Eddie's thoughts began to drift away as his grandpa's words became softer and softer.

When Eddie opened his eyes, his grandfather was gone. And so was his bedroom. He was in a beautiful forest sparkling with a fresh blanket of Christmas snow. Up ahead he saw a clearing where a single present sat alone. He walked over to it and read the gift tag.

To Eddie. What your heart needs most for Christmas.

Curious, Eddie opened the gift. Inside was a handmade Christmas sweater. Eddie was disappointed, but he was so cold that he decided to put it on. It was a perfect fit. Suddenly, the snow around him swirled in all directions, just as if he were inside his snow globe.

When the snow cleared, Eddie discovered that he was sledding with his father. They both laughed and hung on tight as the sled jumped off a small hill and soared through the sky.

"Are you having fun, Eddie?" his father asked.

Eddie looked down at his magical Christmas sweater. "This is the best day ever!" Then Eddie gave his dad a big hug and the snow started to swirl again.

When it settled, Eddie was sitting with his mother at their kitchen table. They had just finished building a gingerbread house. "How did we do?" she asked.

Eddie licked some frosting from his fingers and said, "We're a great team, Mom." He thought about the Christmas sweater he was wearing. Could a simple sweater really have Christmas magic? Suddenly, the snow swirled again.

When it cleared,
Eddie was sitting inside
a sleigh with his grandpa.

"Eddie," Grandpa asked,
"want to take a ride?"

"Sure," Eddie cheered.

"Do I need anything?"

Grandpa hugged him tight and said,

"You've got your Christmas sweater. Looks like you have

everything you'll ever need."

Eddie eyed the candy canes in the sleigh. "Grab one,

Eddie!" With a twinkle in his eye, Grandpa called out to each reindeer by

name and yelled, "Now dash away, dash away, dash away, all!"

The sleigh
lurched forward and
Eddie sat up in his bed.
He'd dreamed the whole night
away. It was Christmas morning and
the smell of his mother's pancakes filled
the house. He jumped out of bed,
scampered downstairs . . .

and stopped dead in his tracks. Under the tree was the bike he'd waited for all year.

But instead of running to it, Eddie slowly searched the room with his eyes.

"Eddie," his mother asked. "Is something wrong?"

"Go ahead and pinch yourself, son," his father said excitedly. "This isn't a dream. Go jump on your new bike!"

Eddie shook his head. "The bike is great, but I was looking for something else."

His family looked at one another with puzzled faces.

With all the sincerity in his heart, he explained, "I was really hoping to get a Christmas sweater. I mean, a bike is just a bike, but a Christmas sweater can be so much more."

Eddie's mom crouched down behind the tree and pulled out a single box. It looked familiar. "Is this what you're searching for?" she asked. Eddie smiled from ear to ear.

He reached for the box, opened it, and eagerly pulled out his Christmas sweater. He stared at it and then put it on over his pajamas. It was a perfect fit. He felt true warmth for the first time in his life.

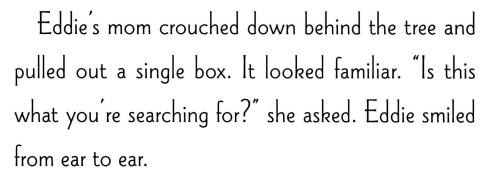

Eddie thought about his dream and about the message on the gift tag.

What your heart needs most for Christmas.

It gave him a magical idea.

He walked over to his mother and gave her the best present in the world——the one thing that her heart also needed the most. . . .

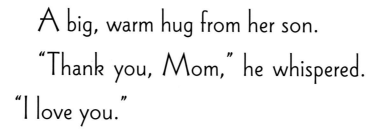

A big, warm hug from her son.

"Thank you, Mom," he whispered.

"I love you."

As Eddie's father looked on proudly, Grandpa picked up a snow globe and gave it a gentle shake. As the flakes settled, he called out to Eddie and, with a familiar twinkle in his eye, slipped a single candy cane into his grandson's pocket.